Thank You, Canada

Andrea Lynn Beck

North Winds Press
An Imprint of Scholastic Canada Ltd.

The illustrations for this book were created using pencil crayon and paint on watercolour paper.

Library and Archives Canada Cataloguing in Publication

Beck, Andrea, author, illustrator
Thank you, Canada / Andrea Lynn Beck.
ISBN 978-1-4431-5723-0 (hardcover)
I. Title.
PS8553.E2948T53 2017   jC813'.54   C2017-901639-3

www.scholastic.ca

6 5 4 3 2 1   Printed in Malaysia 108   17 18 19 20 21

To my girls, Janna and Lins.

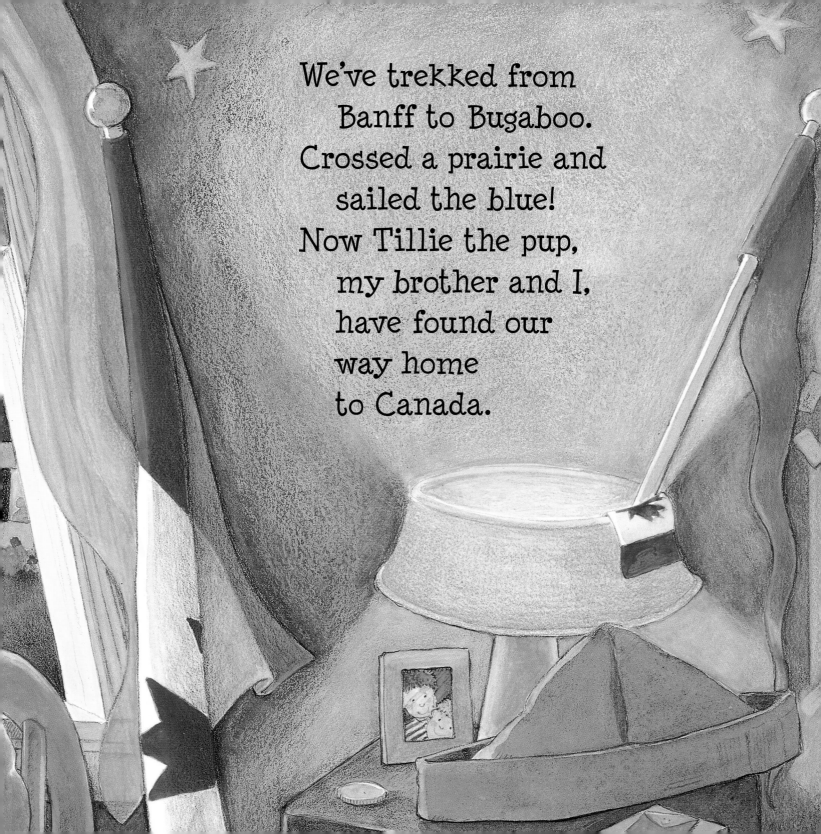

We've trekked from
   Banff to Bugaboo.
Crossed a prairie and
   sailed the blue!
Now Tillie the pup,
   my brother and I,
   have found our
   way home
   to Canada.

I see you out there! Why don't we play?
Tomorrow, perhaps? I'll come your way.
We'll fly to the stars, or snorkel the sea.
We'll roam the Sahara, or climb a big tree.
And then we'll come back to the best place to be.
Thank you, Canada.

Yes! Canada!
We're proud you stretch
from sea to sea,
ten great provinces,
territories, three.
But you're more to us
than geography . . .

English and French
   is a good place to start!
We've many more languages,
   one big heart.

Thank you, Canada,
for our flag.
Our maple leaf up high.

Thank you for our Elders,
and the eagle in the sky.

Thank you, Canada, for our freedoms.
We're proud to be a rainbow!

And thank you for our teachers,
who help us learn and grow.

Thank you, Canada, for our hockey.
Any street or rink will do!

And we won't forget our Forces —
so brave and strong and true!

Thank you, Canada, for our towns
named Love and Tiger Lily.
For Come By Chance and Blow Me Down,
Canadians can be silly.

There's so much more to thank you for:
Sleds, snow, chinooks that blow!
Niagara Falls! Enormous malls!
The loonie and the toonie.
All those giant roadside fish.
My auntie in Antigonish!

There's old Quebec and Stanley Park,
the CN Tower in the dark.
They're all a part of you . . .
the land we love.

But wait!
We can't forget Canada geese!
Royal Canadian Mounted Police!
Beavers, moose, great big spruce.
Lumberjacks, canoes, kayaks.
Polar bears, Arctic hares!
And, *Ooooooo Caaaanadaaaaa*,
   we sing so loud.

Thank you, Canada.
You make us proud.